THE
BRONTOSAURUS
BIRTHDAY CAKE

ROBERT McCRUM
ILLUSTRATED BY MICHAEL FOREMAN

A LITTLE SIMON BOOK
PUBLISHED BY SIMON & SCHUSTER, INC., NEW YORK

Published by LITTLE SIMON, a division of Simon & Schuster, Inc.,
1230 Avenue of the Americas, New York, New York 10020.
First published in Great Britain 1983 by Hamish Hamilton Children's Books.
LITTLE SIMON and colophon are registered trademarks of Simon & Schuster, Inc.
ISBN 0-671-50762-1

Originated and printed in Italy by
Arnoldo Mondadori Editore, Verona

Bobby was seven years old and his head was full of dinosaurs. He thought about tyrannosauruses when he got up in the morning. He imagined meeting pterodactyls on the way to school. And when he came home in the afternoon, his schoolbooks were covered with pre-historic skeletons.

Every night Bobby dreamed about brontosauruses. They were his favorite kind of monster. He knew everything there was to be known about brontosauruses. Bobby had studied the life-size brontosaurus in the museum until he knew it like his best friend.

On Bobby's birthday, there were pink and green and blue packages spread out across the table. There was a book about tyrannosauruses from his aunt. There was a prehistoric jigsaw puzzle from his granny, and a wooden model of a plesiosaurus from his father. And then . . . the lights went out.

Suddenly everyone was singing "Happy Birthday to you," and there was a cake with eight candles blazing away in front of him. When Bobby saw that it was in the shape of a baby brontosaurus, he was over the moon with excitement.

Bobby took a deep breath and blew out the candles.

Bobby looked at the brontosaurus birthday cake.

It seemed a shame to spoil it.

"You must make a wish," said Bobby's mother, handing him the knife.

Bobby laid it gently on the smooth icing. The long neck was a bit like the spout of a teapot. The tail was thin and spiky. The brontosaurus birthday cake was quite fat.

"Don't forget to wish," said his father.

Bobby closed his eyes. He thought: *I wish this brontosaurus was real.* And he started to cut the first slice.

But the knife only just broke the surface. Underneath, it was hard and scaly. Bobby squeezed his eyes shut even tighter and tried again.

Then his mother screamed and his father said, "Good gracious!"

Bobby opened his eyes just in time to see a baby brontosaurus with a perfectly charming smile shake the icing off his back with a wag of his long green tail. Bobby and his family watched in astonishment.

"It's alive!" said his father. "Call the police!"

The brontosaurus scrambled off the plate onto Bobby's knee. He was quite light and, although he had scaly skin, underneath he was soft and warm. Bobby put his arms round him. "He's mine and I shall look after him," Bobby said. "I'm the prehistoric expert round here."

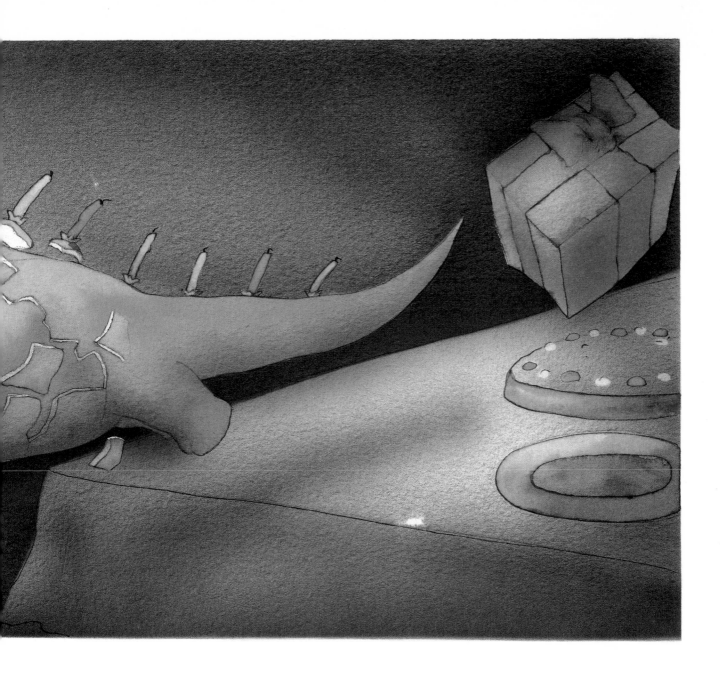

The monster wagged his tail with gratitude and smiled up at Bobby.
Bobby knew very well that brontosauruses have big appetites.
"We must find him something to eat," he said.
Bobby went into the kitchen and the brontosaurus scuttled behind
him. He was about the size of a puppy-dog, and his paws made a
scratchy sound on the floor. Bobby offered him an apple but he
turned up his nose. So he tried cornflakes, then a carrot, then half
a cucumber, a sausage, a lump of cheddar cheese, an orange, a hard-
boiled egg, a piece of toast, some pink Jello, a chocolate eclair, and
finally a dog biscuit.
The brontosaurus looked offended.

Then Bobby caught sight of the peanut butter. He put some peanut butter on a plate on the floor. The brontosaurus sniffed it cautiously and then guzzled the lot with a snort of happiness.

When the dinosaur had finished the whole jar, Bobby saw that he was now twice his original size and showed no signs of stopping. Bobby hoped no one would notice.

As it was Bobby's birthday, he was allowed to stay up late and watch television. The brontosaurus sat with him and watched, too. When it was time to go to bed, the monster was given a box and some straw in the yard outside. That night, Bobby dreamed of real live brontosauruses.

In the morning, Bobby ate his breakfast and went to get his new friend.

"You can't take that thing to school," said his father.

"And I don't want it in the house," said his mother.

So Bobby left the brontosaurus in the backyard. On his way home from school, he did not forget to buy some more peanut butter. He also bought himself a can of Coca-Cola. Soon he was feeding the peanut butter to the dinosaur. But the brontosaurus was looking eagerly at the Coca-Cola.

"Of course," said Bobby. "You're thirsty. Try some."

The brontosaurus swallowed the Coca-Cola in three mouthfuls and looked eagerly about for more. When Bobby's sister, Liz, came home, also with Coca-Cola, the monster drank that as well.

"The brontosaurus is much bigger than he was yesterday," said Liz. "SSSSSSSSSSHHHHHHHHHH!!!!!!!!!!" said Bobby.

But their father had overheard them. "I knew we shouldn't have

kept it," he said with a grunt. "I suppose you think I can afford to have a full-grown mammoth in my house."

"He's not a mammoth," said Bobby.

"Well, they're all fossils to me," said his father with a frown.

The next day the brontosaurus drank a bucket of Coca-Cola and ate six jars of peanut butter.

"I think we should call the police," repeated his father.

"Maybe he'll stop growing," suggested Bobby faintly.

But the brontosaurus grew and grew. His appetite was enormous. One day, he saw Bobby eating a hamburger and fell in love with that, too.

The first time Bobby took the brontosaurus for a walk in the park, no one could believe it was real.

"It's a real one, all right," he said. "A real live brontosaurus."

Soon the brontosaurus was the talk of the neighborhood. Everyone wanted to see the amazing celebrity. He was filmed for television and featured in the newspapers.

"You may have been a paleolithic has-been," said Bobby affectionately, "but you're certainly the talk of the town."

The brontosaurus gave a protozoic smile as if to say, "Well, what do you expect from a real live brontosaurus?"

Huge crowds began to gather in the local park to see the brontosaurus and his master playing soccer on the grass. The mayor was not pleased. The crowds trampled on the flowers in the park. Besides, the mayor wanted to make money out of the brontosaurus.

When Bobby had finished exercising his pet, he would lead him through the twilit streets, followed by a mass of curious spectators. Bobby's house was suddenly famous.

"I wish these people would go away," said his mother.

Just then there was the sound of a siren and a police car drew up.

"I knew all this nonsense was against the law," said Bobby's father.

"I understand from my inquiries," the policeman said, "that you have a Brontosaurus on the premises."

"That's right," said Bobby's mother, who, unlike her husband, had become quite fond of the monster.

"I would like to inspect the animal in question," said the policeman.

"You can't take him away!" Bobby protested.

"We'll see about that," said the policeman with a stern look. "Where is it?"

"In the garage," said Bobby's father, who was not happy having to park his car in the street.

"How he's grown!" said Bobby's mother with pride.

The policeman took one look at the brontosaurus and went very white. Then he hurried outside and slammed the door.

"Th—th—th—that animal's against the l—l—l—law," he said.

"He's very tame," said Bobby with a smile. "He started life as a birthday cake."

"I don't care where he started," said the policeman. "It's where he's got to that worries me." He looked sternly at Bobby. "How much more growing has he got to do?"

Quick as a flash, Bobby replied, "A fully grown brontosaurus is fifty feet high and seventy feet long and weighs about fifty policemen."

"That settles it," said the policeman. "I'm calling the zoo."

So the brontosaurus was given a special cage in the local zoo. One of the first visitors was the mayor, who looked very pleased. "At last my town has a tourist attraction all its own," he said, greedily.

And he was right. Crowds of children and their parents arrived every day. Every morning there were terrific lines to get in. The zoo keeper built special seats outside the brontosaurus's cage so that he could charge extra money.

Every day after school, Bobby visited the monster in his cage to make sure he was happy. Every day he watched him eat his evening meal of hamburgers, peanut butter, and Coca-Cola.

The brontosaurus was now fifty feet tall and seventy feet long, as Bobby had predicted. And when he stepped onto the zoo keeper's weighing machine he came to exactly fifty policemen. His scales were perfectly green. His long neck stretched out in front of him like a giraffe's and his tail was so strong that Bobby could go for rides on it.

"To think," said Bobby happily, "that you were once a birthday cake."

But then Bobby noticed huge green tears in the monster's eyes, running down his long neck and falling splash—splash—splash onto the straw in his cage. The brontosaurus was crying.

"Why are you so unhappy?" Bobby asked. "You have all the Coca-Cola and hamburgers you could want. There will be no short-age of peanut butter, I promise. You are famous,primeval old timer. What more do you want?"

The brontosaurus looked at him with big wide eyes and pointed his neck toward the door of his cage.

Then Bobby understood. "You want to be free," he said. The bron-

tosaurus waved his great green neck up and down in agreement.

Bobby went home filled with great sadness. "I must talk to the mayor," he said to himself.

But the mayor was very cross when he heard what Bobby had to say. "Stuff and nonsense," he said. "I've never heard anything like it. All the animals in the zoo are happy. You ask them. Besides, the brontosaurus is good for business."

"But he's not happy," said Bobby.

"We'll soon see about that," said the mayor. "Come with me, boy."

So he and the mayor set off in the mayor's official car for the zoo. But when they arrived there was a terrible fuss going on.

"OH! OH! OH!" the zoo keeper was shouting. People were running about with ropes and ladders. "What shall I do?" cried the zoo keeper.

"What's the matter?" asked the mayor.

"Haven't you heard? The brontosaurus has ESCAPED!"

The mayor went pale. "ESCAPED!!!" he shouted. "Well, don't stand there! Do something! Find it—OR WE ARE ALL RUINED!!!!"

The police went zooming around in squad cars with their sirens going full blast. The fire department was called out, and the firemen

sprayed water in all directions. Special detectives put on prehistoric disguises and went out looking for the brontosaurus. AN APPEAL FROM THE MAYOR was broadcast on the radio and television. And a REWARD of ONE THOUSAND DOLLARS was offered to the first person who found the brontosaurus alive.

Bobby was pleased. "At least my antediluvian friend is free," he said to himself, "wherever he is."

Days passed. The brontosaurus was nowhere to be found. Some people said that he had fled abroad. Other people said that he was hiding in the nearby forest, or in the city sewers. Others said he was dead.

The mayor grew more and more frantic. No one went to the zoo anymore. The reward was increased to TWO THOUSAND DOLLARS.

Secretly, Bobby and his friends were pleased. Everyone knew that the way the mayor had made money out of the brontosaurus wasn't fair.

One night Bobby was lying in bed when he heard a knock at the window. He jumped up. There was the familiar face of the brontosaurus peering in through the window.

He rushed downstairs to get the brontosaurus off the street before the police saw him. He led his friend into the backyard.

"Welcome home, errant fossil," Bobby said affectionately.

The brontosaurus wagged his tail and nodded.

Bobby could hardly sleep for excitement and worry. What was he going to do with his massive pet? There was no way he could hide him in the garage or the garden. People would soon find out and try to claim the reward. How could he stop the brontosaurus from being taken back to the mayor's zoo?

Bobby lay awake with this puzzle and watched the stars move across the sky. Gradually an idea took shape in his mind.

It was still dark when he crept downstairs into the garden. "PSSSTT!" he called out.

But the brontosaurus was already awake, shivering in the cold.

"You can't stay here," he said. "You'll end up in the zoo. That mayor's not to be trusted."

The brontosaurus nodded his head. "So I'm going to tell the mayor I've found you."

The dinosaur looked surprised.

"Don't worry. By the time he hears, you'll be miles away, in the secret places you've been hiding all these weeks. I know all there is to know about you. Popping up in birthday cakes is not your only trick."

The monster looked a bit sheepish, as if to say, "Well, you're right,

of course." Bobby placed a hand on the scaly shoulder and looked up at the sky. It was getting light. "Now off you go."

The brontosaurus looked at him sadly.

"I shall miss you too, but it's better this way. I'll always know where to find you." Bobby smiled. "Cheer up. The mayor will never find you."

The brontosaurus, with a shake of his big green tail, lumbered over

the garden fence and disappeared into the dawn.

When they got up for breakfast, Bobby's mother and father were astonished to hear the news.

"You've found the brontosaurus!" they exclaimed.

"Where is it?" asked his father. "I'm calling the police."

"No you're not," said Bobby firmly. "Because he's not here. He's gone away again—and I'm the only one who knows where he is.

"And now I must go and see the mayor," he said, and rushed
off to the town hall.

The mayor came hurrying out of the town hall, surrounded by all
of his people, very excited. "Well, well, well," said the mayor, patting
Bobby on the head. "So we've found the brontosaurus, have we?"

"Yes," said Bobby.

"Well, come on." The mayor was stern. "Tell us where it is. I

haven't got all day, you know."

Bobby looked steadily at the mayor. "The brontosaurus doesn't like the way you do things around here. He's decided he will never come back."

The mayor and all the people from the town hall stared at each other in astonishment. "Never come back!" they exclaimed.

"That's right," said Bobby. "I'm the only one who knows where he

is." He smiled. "And I intend to keep it a secret."

The mayor looked very cross and pompous. "You realize, young man, that you're waving good–bye to Two Thousand Dollars."

"That's fine by me," said Bobby.

The mayor knew he was beaten. "I suppose all good things have to come to an end sometime," he sighed.

Life isn't quite the same as before, but at least Bobby and his

friends all know that the brontosaurus is free and happy. And anyway, there's really no telling when he might burst back into their lives . . .

And from time to time, Bobby and the brontosaurus have secret

meetings in unlikely places. If you catch sight of them on a deserted beach, or off the beaten track in the countryside, or even late at night in an empty parking lot, you'll remember to keep it to yourself, won't you?